Chester Raccoon
AND THE
Acorn Full of Memories

By Audrey Penn
Illustrated by Barbara L. Gibson

Tanglewood • Terre Haute, IN

Published by Tanglewood Publishing, Inc., August 2009.

Text © 2009 Audrey Penn
Illustrations © 2009 Barbara Leonard Gibson

Design by Amy Alick Perich

Tanglewood Publishing, Inc.
P. O. Box 3009
Terre Haute, IN 47803

www.tanglewoodbooks.com

Printed in China
10 9 8 7 6 5 4 3 2 1

ISBN 978-1-933718-29-3

Library of Congress Cataloging-in-Publication Data

Penn, Audrey, 1947-
  Chester Raccoon and the acorn full of memories / by Audrey Penn;
illustrated by Barbara L. Gibson.
        p. cm.
  Summary: After his mother explains why his classmate is not
returning to school, she teaches Chester Raccoon how to make a memory.
  ISBN 978-1-933718-29-3
  [1. Memory--Fiction. 2. Death--Fiction. 3. Grief--Fiction. 4.
Mother and child--Fiction. 5. Raccoon--Fiction. 6. Forest animals--
Fiction.] I. Gibson, Barbara, ill. II. Title.
  PZ7.P38448Ch 2009
  [E]--dc22
                        2009013734

For Thistle, Shadow, Lemur, Chloe, and Tary. You were loyal and loving and our best friends. We will love you and remember you in our hearts forever. Your water bowls are always filled.
-AP

For Mom, Dad and Karen...
three acorns and many, many memories.
-BG

C hester Raccoon climbed into his tree hollow and frowned. "Skiddil Squirrel didn't come to school today," he told his mother.

"Owl Teacher said he had an accident and wouldn't be coming back. What's an accident?"

"An accident is something that happens that isn't supposed to happen," explained Mrs. Raccoon. She lifted Chester onto her lap and folded her warm, loving arms around him. "Did Owl Teacher say anything else about Skiddil Squirrel? Did she say he died?"

"I think so," said Chester. "But I don't know what that means either."

Mrs. Raccoon thought for a moment. "Do you remember what happened to old Mr. Beaver?"

Chester nodded. "His heart quit beating and his body didn't work any more."

"That's right," Mrs. Raccoon told him. "That's what happens when somebody dies." She put a comforting arm around Chester's shoulders. "That's what happened when Skiddil Squirrel died."

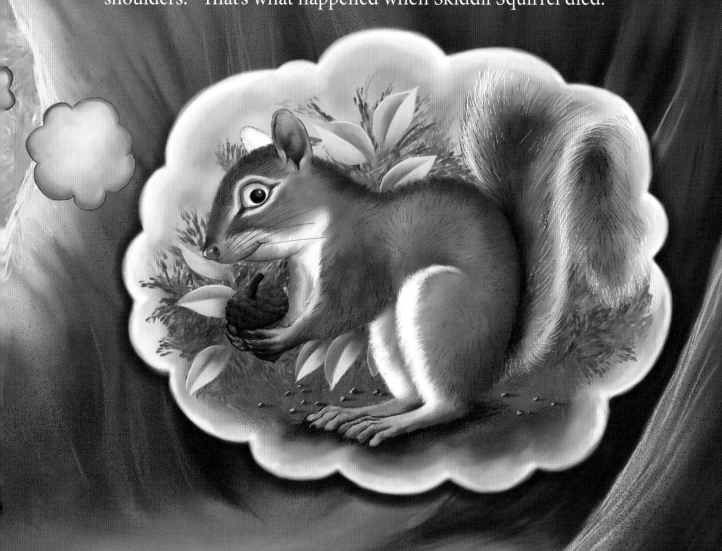

"Oh." Now that Chester understood what happened to Skiddil Squirrel, his insides felt jumbled and he was very sad. Mrs. Raccoon gently stroked the top of his head. "I'm very sorry about Skiddil Squirrel, Chester."

Chester turned and faced his mother. "Skiddil Squirrel is my friend and I want to play with him," he cried. "Why won't his body work? Why doesn't his heart beat?"

"I'm afraid that's one of those questions no forest animal can answer. It's like asking 'Who lights up the sun then blows it out?' or 'Who collects the pieces of the moon when it disappears, then puts the pieces back when it's full?' I know what you can do! Why don't you make a memory of Skiddil Squirrel? That way, you'll never forget him."

"How do you make a memory?" asked Chester.

"You begin by finding something that reminds you of him, the way your piece of tree bark reminds you of the hollow where we used to live."

"I'd rather have Skiddil Squirrel than something that reminds me of him," sniffled Chester.

"I know you would," soothed his mother. "And I know how much you'll miss him. But making a memory of him will help." She lifted Chester off her lap and wrapped his tiny hands in hers. "Tell me what Skiddil Squirrel liked."

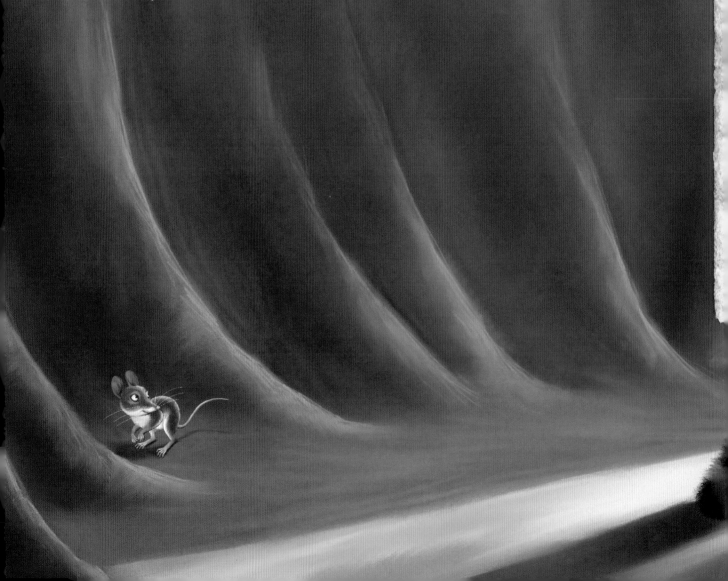

"He liked butterflies," Chester said thoughtfully, "and acorns!"
"Butterflies and acorns," his mother repeated out loud. "And where was Skiddil Squirrel's favorite place to play?"
"The butterfly pond."

Mrs. Raccoon bent down and kissed Chester on his forehead. Chester's ears twitched and his muzzle blushed.

"Let's go see if butterflies and acorns can help us make a memory of Skiddil Squirrel, shall we?" she asked him. She led Chester outside, picked up his little brother Ronny who had his curious little nose inside an anthill, and walked the two cubs down the wooded path toward the butterfly pond.

On their way to the pond, Chester's best friend Cassy popped out from behind her tree. "Where are you going?" she asked Chester.

"We're going to the butterfly pond to make a memory of Skiddil Squirrel. Want to come?"

"Okay. But I don't know how to make a memory."

"You find something like my piece of tree bark, only it's not tree bark because it has to do with butterflies and acorns, and it's something that reminds you of Skiddil Squirrel."

"I can do that," said Cassy.

As the four raccoons scurried toward the pond, more and more of Skiddil Squirrel's friends asked if they, too, could come along and make a memory. Before long, two deer, six skunks, three opossums, fourteen rabbits, Badger, a bluebird, six mourning doves, a green snake, twenty-two mice, four squirrels, a beaver, and two chipmunks walked, crawled, slithered, hopped, and flew to the edge of the pond.

"I've never seen so many butterflies!" chittered Mrs. Raccoon when they arrived. There were butterflies, and butterflies, and more butterflies! Butterflies were everywhere. They were over the pond, in the trees, under the bushes, on the flowers, and resting on single blades of grass between the animals' feet.

"What do I do now?" asked Chester as a bright purple butterfly balanced on the tip of his nose.

"Tell me a story about Skiddil Squirrel," said Mrs. Raccoon.
"What kind of a story?"
"Something that happened here at the pond."

Chester scrunched his nose thoughtfully and the butterfly flew away. "Once when we were playing here, about a gazillion butterflies landed on Skiddil Squirrel all at the same time. He was so covered in butterflies, you could hardly see his fur! He thought that with all those butterflies standing on him, he could fly like they do.

So he took a running start and jumped into the air when he got to the edge of the pond. He landed SPLASH on his belly and all the butterflies flew off. He dripped all the way back to his tree."

"That's a wonderful memory," laughed Mrs. Raccoon.
"Do you have another one?"

"One day Skiddil Squirrel made us all late for school because a caterpillar was turning into a butterfly, and he wouldn't let us miss it. We all watched the butterfly come out of its chrysalis and spread open its brand new wings. Skiddil Squirrel was so excited, he told all the other butterflies what happened even though they already knew."

"That's a lovely memory," agreed Chester's mother.

Suddenly Chester looked sad. "One day after school, Skiddil Squirrel came here and buried all of the acorns he had collected for the winter. But when he wanted them, he forgot where he had buried them. He really loved those acorns. Everyone in school helped him look for them."

"Did he find them?" asked Mrs. Raccoon.

Chester shook his head. "No."

Mrs. Raccoon stood up on her back legs and looked around. She spotted a hillside not far away and patted Chester on the top of his head. "I think I know where those acorns are buried," she told him. She pointed to a small group of brand new oak trees growing at the base of the hillside.

"Those are Skiddil Squirrel trees!" shouted Chester when he saw the young trees for himself. "The forest made a Skiddil Squirrel memory!"

"I believe it did," said Mrs. Raccoon. "Those trees, your stories, and the butterflies all make wonderful memories of Skiddil Squirrel."

Chester suddenly noticed a beautiful black-and-orange butterfly on the ground beside his front foot. When it folded its wings, he saw the acorn beneath it. He gently and carefully lifted the acorn and butterfly off the ground, held his breath, and waited patiently until the butterfly flew away on its own. He clutched the acorn in his front paw and looked up at his mother.

"This acorn is the memory I'll take home," he told her. "I'll
keep it with my special piece of tree bark. Every time I look at it,
I'll think of Skiddil Squirrel."

"It's a beautiful acorn, Chester. It will make a perfect memory."

With the acorn securely clutched in his paw, Chester scampered over to the Skiddil Squirrel trees and placed a Kissing Hand on each new tree trunk.

"I'll never forget you, Skiddil Squirrel. Thank you for being my friend!"